PAY ATTENTION, EMILY BROWN!

Written by Linda Burton

Illustrated by Carl Burton

Would you please pay attention, Miss Emily Brown?

You've looked in...

and this bee...

Now, Emily Brown, would you *please* look at me?

Where are you,

Did you stroll into town?

Are you sliding down mountains,

There is one thing I know...

You are not here with me!

Perhaps you can't see me, Miss Emily Brown...

Should I paint myself red?

Should I put on a crown?

Should I light myself up like a bright Christmas tree?

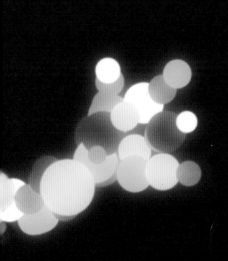

Please, Emily Brown, pay attention to me!

I know! You can't hear me!

Right, Emily Brown?

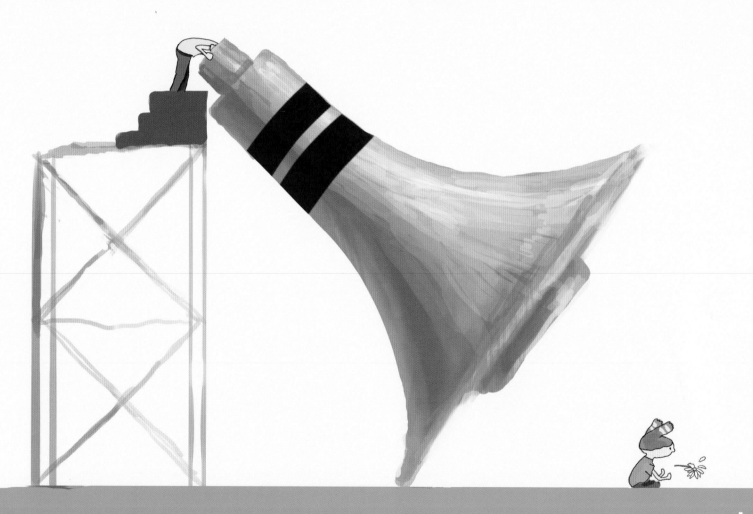

I'll go buy a foghorn to make a big sound.

Or maybe some cymbals would just guarantee
(if I added some drums)
that you'd listen to me.

Just think, Emmy Brown, for a moment or two...

Suppose that I told you my toes had turned blue?

Suppose that I started to fly overhead?

Or spread candy and presents all over your bed?

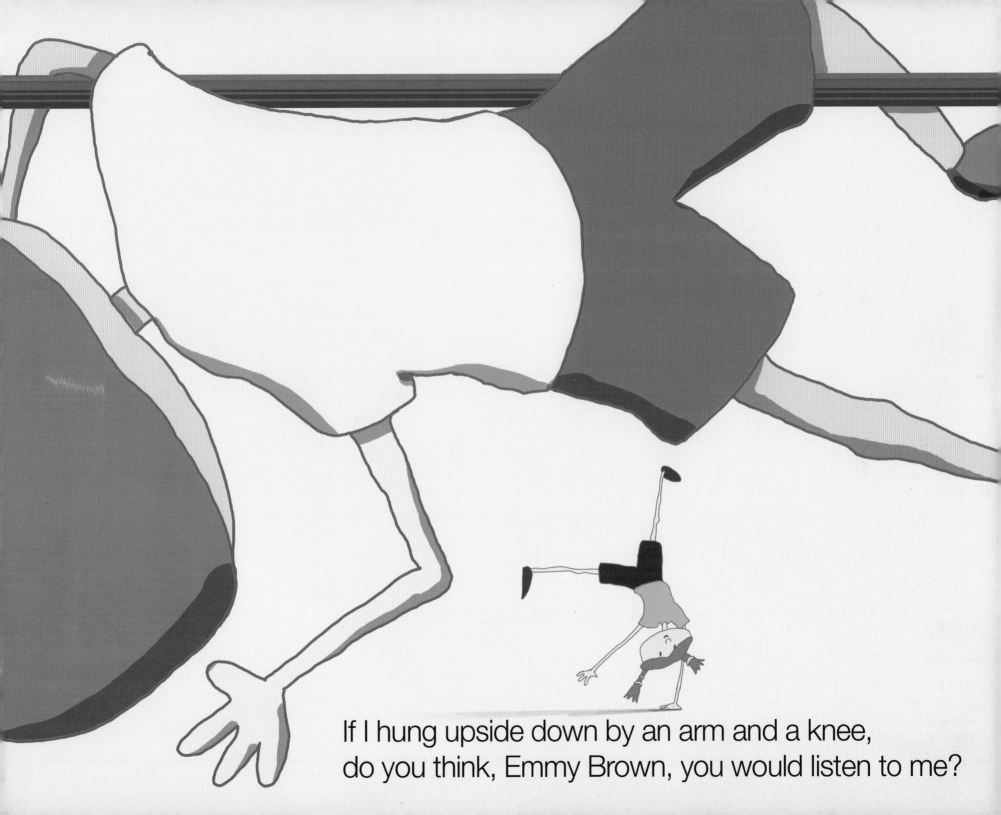

If I hung upside down by an arm and a knee,
do you think, Emmy Brown, you would listen to me?

to turn your attention a little my way?

Or maybe a hug and a kiss would go far

to show you I want you the way that you are.

For whatever you don't or whatever you do,

I love you so much, you lovable you.

Linda Burton has been, for four decades, the biological, foster, and adoptive mother of children with attentional/behavioral deficits, ranging from mild to profound. This hands-on experience has taught her that diagnoses such as ADHD, autism, and Asperger's are most successfully addressed when emphasis is placed on humor, love, and acceptance. A contributing columnist for the former New York Times Syndicate, her writing on the topic of family and education has appeared in *Reader's Digest, Family Circle, The Wall Street Journal,* and many other major newspapers and magazines. Linda Burton is an experienced public speaker, has made many national TV and radio appearances, and has testified before Congress on alternatives to daycare. Now living with her family in Central Illinois, she is a native Virginian.

Carl Burton is an artist with a special interest in experimental animation. He lives and works in New York City.